ÉGALITÈ

Candy Pink
Egalité Series

© Text: Adela Turin, 1976
© Illustrations: Nella Bosnia, 1976
© Edition: NubeOcho, 2016
www.nubeocho.com – info@nubeocho.com

Original title:
Rosaconfetto © Dalla parte delle bambine, Milan, 1976
Rose Bonbon © Actes Sud, 1999, 2008, 2014

English translation: Martin Hyams
Text editing: Caroline Dookie

Distributed in the United States by
Consortium Book Sales & Distribution

First Edition: 2016
ISBN: 978-84-944318-9-0
Printed in China

Candy Pink

ADELA TURIN   NELLA BOSNIA

Once upon a time, in elephant country, there was
a herd of elephants in which the females had large
bright eyes and skin the color of candy pink.

The little girl elephants got this beautiful
color because, from the time they were born,
they only ate anemones and peonies.

It's not that anemones and peonies
were very nutritious...

...but they made their skin smooth and pink, and their eyes bright and beautiful.

The anemones and peonies grew in a little walled garden. Enclosed within, the little girl elephants played together and ate the flowers.

"Little girls", said their dads, "if you don't eat your anemones and finish your peonies, you'll never be as beautiful and pink as your mommies.
You'll never have bright eyes, and no one will want to marry you when you are older."

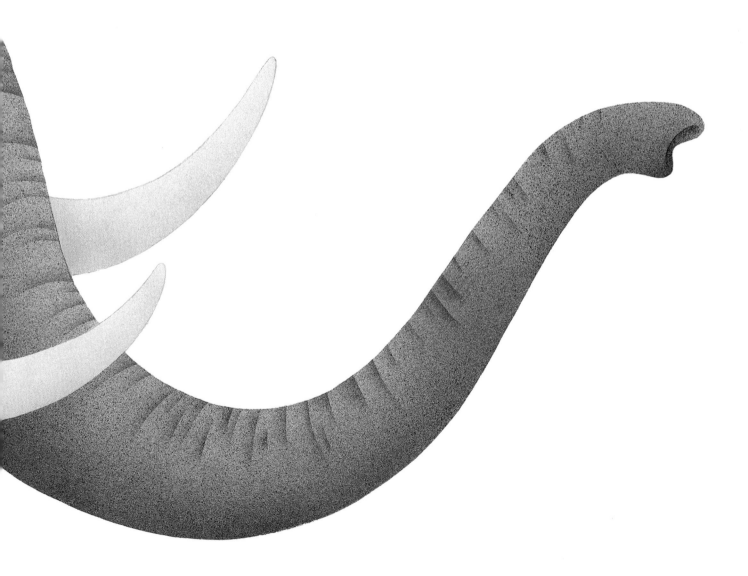

To make the pink color
come out more,
the parents dressed their
daughters in pink shoes and
pink collar bibs and tied
pink ribbons on their tails.

While the little girl elephants stayed in the
walled garden with the peonies and anemones,
they watched their brothers and boy cousins, all
of them gray elephants, playing in the fragrant
savannah, eating green grass, wallowing in water
and mud, and napping under the trees.

Daisy was slightly different from the other girl
elephants. Even though she ate her peonies and
anemones, she was the only little elephant that
didn't turn pink, not even a hint.

This made her mom very sad and
greatly annoyed her dad.

"But Daisy," they said, " why do you still
have this ugly gray color that simply
doesn't suit a little girl elephant?
Are you doing it on purpose?
Perhaps you want to be a rebel?"

"Listen, Daisy! If you carry on
like this, you´ll never be
a beautiful female elephant."

Daisy, becoming grayer and grayer
every day, just kept quiet.
But to make her parents happy, she
ate another mouthful of anemones
and another one of peonies.

Daisy's parent's eventually abandoned all hope of her becoming pink and beautiful, with big bright eyes, like every female elephant should be.

They decided to leave her in peace.

Daisy felt so relieved. She left the enclosure and
got rid of her pink shoes, her pink collar bib,
and the pink ribbon tied to her tail.
She wandered off on her own in the tall grass,
under the trees laden with delicious fruit,
and wallowed in the lovely muddy puddles.

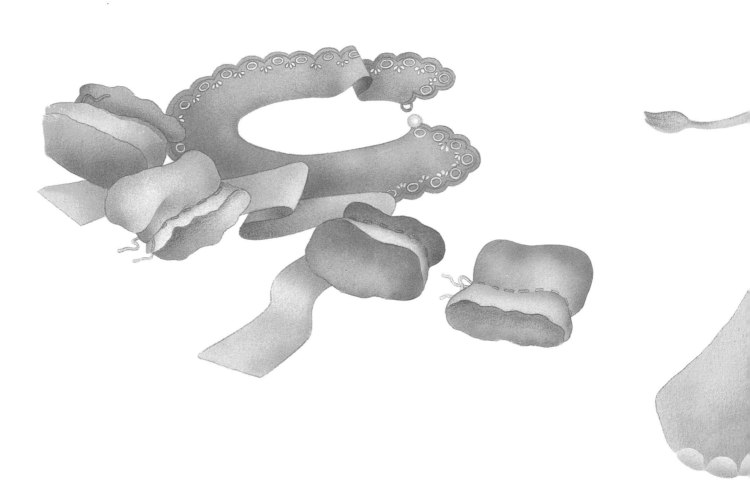

From the walled garden,
the other little girl elephants watched.
The first day they felt frightened;
the second day worried;
the third day bewildered,
and the fourth day jealous.

On the fifth day, one by one,
the bravest began to leave the enclosure.
Shoes, bibs and ribbons lay abandoned in piles all
around the garden of peonies and anemones.

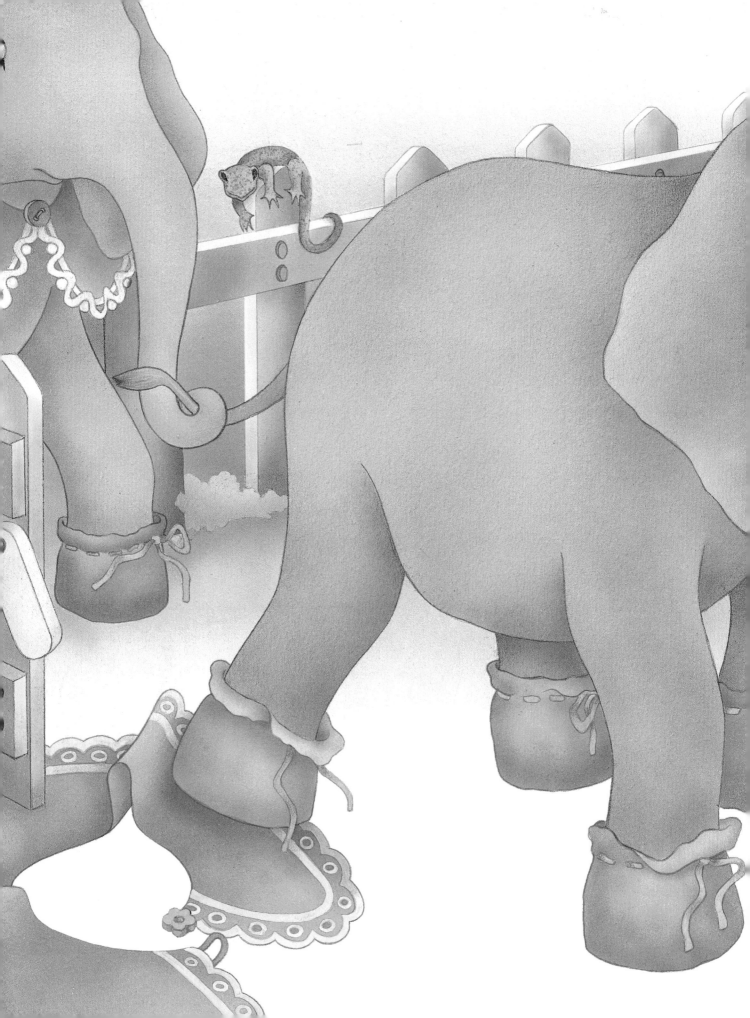

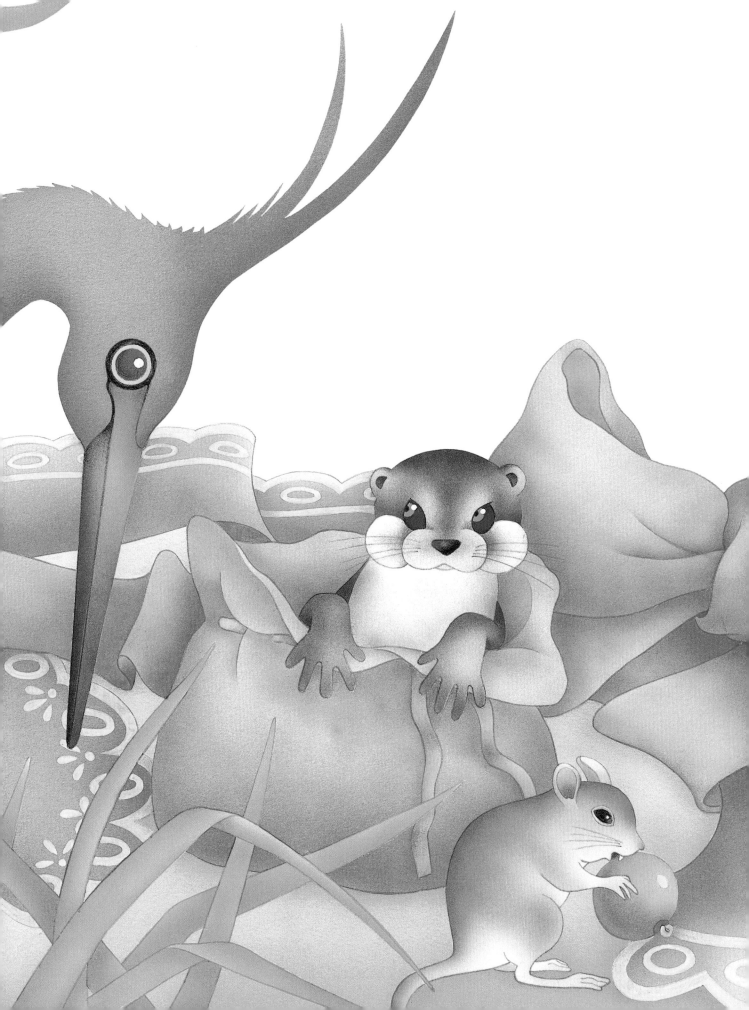

After tasting the green grass and the tasty fruit,
feeling the cool breeze, playing joyful games,
taking naps under the shade of leafy trees,
none of the little girl elephants ever wanted to see
a shoe or eat a peony, let alone stay in a walled garden.

And ever since then,
it's been hard to tell the difference
between boy elephants and girl elephants.